EGMONT
We bring stories to life

This edition published in Great Britain 2010 by Dean,
an imprint of Egmont UK Limited
239 Kensington High Street, London W8 6SA
All Rights Reserved

HiT entertainment

ISBN 978 0 6035 6523 6
1 3 5 7 9 10 8 6 4 2
Printed and bound in Italy

Thomas and the
Green Controller

It was a quiet day at Tidmouth Sheds. Percy was all alone.

Suddenly, Lady Hatt and her friends arrived at the Sheds.

"The Fat Controller is sick," she announced. "He has lost his voice."

Percy was worried. "I hope he finds it soon," he peeped.

Lady Hatt read out a list of jobs from The Fat Controller. "Gordon is to collect coaches of china from Knapford and take them to the Docks . . . he must go very slowly."

"Slow cars," peeped Percy.

"James is to shunt trucks in the Coal Yards . . . he must be as busy as a bee," Lady Hatt went on.

"Busy bee!" puffed Percy.

"And Toby is to take visitors to the Scottish Castle . . . he must go as fast as Gordon's Express!"

"Gordon's Express," puffed Percy.

"You're in charge now, Percy," said Lady Hatt.

Thomas puffed in to the sheds.

"I'm Controller for the day,"
peeped Percy, proudly.

"Do you need any help?" Thomas
asked his friend.

"No, thank you, Controllers don't
need help!" wheeshed Percy.

And off he chuffed.

Percy found Gordon first.
"The Fat Controller has lost his
voice," puffed Percy. "So I am the
Controller today."

Gordon was surprised.

Percy tried hard to remember what
Lady Hatt had said. "You must pull
very slow cars!" he peeped.

"Oh, the indignity!" huffed Gordon.

Percy had a lot to do and a lot
to remember!

Next, Percy found James at
the Washdown.

"James, you must be a busy bee!"
he peeped.

James gasped. "Do you mean
I have to be yellow and black?"
he whistled.

"Yes, James," Percy said, sternly.

James wanted to keep his red paint!

"Engines must do as they are told,"
Percy boomed, as he puffed away.

Next, Percy found Toby. "Toby, you must pull Gordon's Express!" he told him.

"Why?" Toby asked. He was very puzzled by this new task.

"That's your job, you must do as you are told" peeped Percy, loudly.

Percy felt very important.

Later, Percy decided it was time
to check on all his engines.

He knew that is what The Fat
Controller would do.

Some children were waiting on the
bridge to see the engines.

"Hello!" Percy peeped.

But the children were looking
at the track where Gordon was
puffing slowly down the line.

The children began to laugh.
"Look at Gordon," they cried.
"What a slowcoach!"

Then James arrived at the signal.
The children started to laugh again.

James' splendid red paintwork
was not splendid or red any more,
he had been painted with yellow
and black stripes!

"Who is that giant stripey bee?"
the children called.

Finally, Toby the Tram Engine huffed in with the heavy Express.

It was very hard work for a little engine like him, and Toby was tired.

"My axles ache!" poor Toby wheeshed to James.

Gordon, James and Toby heard the children laughing.

Percy was watching, anxiously.

Gordon called out to Percy,
"I am supposed to be the fastest
engine on Sodor! Not the slowest!"
he huffed.

"I'm supposed to be the reddest engine on Sodor," moaned James. "Now no one knows who I am!"

"I'm only a steam tram," Toby puffed. "The Express is just too heavy for me to pull."

Percy was worried. He knew he had made lots of mistakes.

Just then, Thomas puffed alongside Percy. "What is wrong?" he asked his friend.

"Please help me, Thomas. I can't remember what Lady Hatt told me. All the engines are doing the wrong jobs."

Thomas thought for a moment. "You must go back over your tracks," he said. "You might see things that will help you remember."

Percy thought that was a very good idea.

First, Thomas and Percy chuffed
into Knapford Station.

"Gordon and slow cars," puffed
Percy to himself.

Suddenly, Percy saw crates of china waiting on the platform.

"That's it!" Percy cried. "Gordon is to take the china to the Docks. He must pull his coaches very slowly!"

Then, Percy and Thomas puffed
into the Coal Yards.

"James must be a busy bee,"
Percy said, slowly.

There were lots of grumbling coal trucks waiting to be shunted.

"That's it – James has to shunt lots of trucks! So, he must be as busy as a bee!" peeped Percy, happily.

Finally, Percy and Thomas arrived
at the station.

"Toby must pull Gordon's Express,"
puzzled Percy.

Suddenly, Percy saw a group of visitors, waiting on the platform.

"That's it!" he cried. "Toby is to take visitors to the Scottish Castle! He has to go as fast as Gordon's Express!"

Later, when the The Fat Controller was feeling better, he visited the engines in the Sheds.

"You have done well, little Percy," he smiled. "I'm very pleased."

"And I'm very pleased that you've found your voice." Percy tooted, happily. "I just hope you never lose it again!"